Come, Meet
JACOB,
The Grabbing Twin

Come, Meet
JACOB,
The Grabbing Twin

The Story of Genesis 28—31

Kitty Anna Griffiths

Illustrated by "Willy"

ZONDERVAN
PUBLISHING HOUSE

OF THE ZONDERVAN CORPORATION | GRAND RAPIDS, MICHIGAN 49506

Books in the COME, MEET series:

Adam and Eve
Noah
Abraham, the Pioneer
Abraham, God's Friend
Isaac
Jacob, the Grabbing Twin
Jacob, God's Prince
Joseph, God's Dreamer
Joseph, the Grand Vizier
Ruth
Jesus, the Baby
Jesus, the Boy

All the above books are on cassette, as are many other stories, all told by the author with music and sound effects. They are obtainable from "A Visit With Mrs. G.," Box 179, Station J, Toronto, Ontario, Canada.

COME, MEET JACOB, THE GRABBING TWIN
© 1978 by Kitty Anna Griffiths
First Zondervan edition - 1978

Library of Congress Cataloging in Publication Data
Griffiths, Kitty Anna.
    Come, meet Jacob, the grabbing twin.

    (Come, meet stories)
    SUMMARY: Tells of the travels of Jacob and his marriages to Leah and Rachel.
    1. Jacob, the patriarch—Juvenile literature.   2. Bible stories, English—O.T. Genesis.   3. Bible. O.T.—Biography—Juvenile literature.   4. Patriarchs (Bible)—Biography—Juvenile literature. [1. Jacob, the patriarch.   2. Bible stories—O.T.] I. Title.
BS580.J3G75   222'.11'09505   78-18458
ISBN 0-310-25271-7

To David

with love

Contents

Preface

This book continues the story of the rivalry between Jacob and Esau, the twin sons of Isaac and Rebekah. You can read about their early struggles in Mrs. G.'s book *Come, Meet Isaac.*

Jacob and Esau were born fighting. Esau was born first by a few minutes and was thus the eldest son. Yet God had told the twins' mother, Rebekah, that *Jacob* was the one who should receive all the special blessings promised to his grandfather Abraham, and his father Isaac. It was *Jacob,* not Esau, who should lead God's people through the next stage of His plan for them.

Isaac always thought of Esau as his heir, and Esau was undoubtedly his favorite. Rebekah was painfully aware of this situation, and in desperation she decided God needed help from her to arrange that the right son get the blessing. She persuaded Jacob to deceive his blind father, Isaac, into thinking he was Esau. Jacob got the coveted blessing. But Rebekah got a pack of trouble. Isaac was deeply distressed, Esau was so furious he vowed he'd kill his brother, and Jacob had to flee for his life.

Rebekah was faced with a problem. No one must suspect that God's "chosen one" was running away. How much better to say that Jacob was leaving home in search of a wife—a wife who would be a suitable helpmeet for God's chosen leader. And such a wife could only be found among her relatives in Haran.

Mrs. G. invites you to *Come, Meet Jacob, the Grabbing Twin.*

JACOB LEAVES HOME

TO HARAN
AND THE WELL OF
THE MAGIC WORDS

MEDITERRANEAN
GREAT SEA

JACOB
MEETS
RACHEL
AT THE WELL

BETHEL

THE CAVE OF
MACHPELAH
WHERE
ABRAHAM
AND SARAH
WERE

MAMRE

SALT
SEA

HEBRON
JACOB'S
HOME

FATHER ISAAC
FARMED HERE

1

The Shining Ladder

Jacob left home like a hero, setting out to find a wife, with Isaac's magnificent blessing still ringing in his ears. Not the blessing he'd gotten yesterday when he'd dressed up and pretended to be Esau, his brother, but the beautiful blessing he'd had this very morning from his father, with all the camp listening.

The blessing ended: "May God give you the blessing of Abraham! And may He give you the land that He promised to Abraham." Wow! "The blessing of Abraham!" Now, for sure, Jacob was recognized as God's chosen one. And this was very important to Jacob.

It had been awful saying good-by to Rebekah, his mother. Rebekah had tried to be brave, but he knew she'd miss him terribly. Her life had been wrapped up in Jacob for forty years. Jacob was no spring chicken, was he? But, of course, you remember life was different in those days, and forty was a good marriageable age for a man. Anyway, his mother said she'd let him know as soon as it was safe for him to come home again. He'd have a wife with him then—hopefully.

Yes, when it was safe for him to come back, back he'd come—when Esau had stopped being angry, when Esau had stopped wanting to kill him. His mother had said, "Stay a few days with Uncle Laban."

Esau had been standing there this morning among the well-wishers, terribly sorry to see his twin brother leaving. He'd looked very thoughtful. He'd been amazed that Jacob should go to such lengths to look for the right sort of wife when, to his mind, there were lots of lovely girls around home. I think Esau would have been more amazed to know that Jacob was fleeing for his life—from him!

Jacob was traveling light and alone. He had his small pack, his water bottle (for drinking water), some bread, dried meat and nuts, and his stick. And a few extra clothes in his pack, of course.

He had no fancy "labola" (bridal price) to offer the father of the girl he hoped to find and marry. "I guess I'll just have to work to pay for her," he said.

Jacob had gotten what he'd wanted—the blessing of the eldest son, the inheritance. Two blessings still rang in his ears. The one he'd gotten by dishonesty yesterday had made it necessary for him to run for his life from his angry brother Esau. But the other blessing, freely given him this morning by his father, had made him look like a conquering hero leaving home. Things aren't always what they appear, are they?

Jacob had thought and thought all day till his head ached. "The moment I got what I wanted—and *how* I'd wanted it—I had to leave it behind me and run for my life. But who's to know that?"

When Jacob got ready for bed that night he was a whole day's journey away from home. He was all alone in wild, rocky country. The sun had set. Owls hooted and shrieked around him. Bats swooped close to him—just missing his hair. Oh, what was that? A big owl flew very close.

Its great wing swished his shoulder.

Hyenas laughed in the distance. Jackals howled, and the ground fairly shook when a lion roared. And it wasn't too far away either!

Jacob felt a little nervous.

All these sounds echoed round the rocks. Luz was a rocky place, and it just happened that Luz was as far as he'd traveled by sundown.

No place was safe, really. Wild animals roamed and prowled everywhere. And, of course, the night birds' hooting and screeching were enough to bother anybody.

Jacob was so tired that he could have slept on a clothesline, or so he thought. He draped a cloth over a big smooth stone to make a pillow. Oh, dear! Camping out was so new to Jacob. He loved the comforts of home, but now he wrapped himself in his cloak and, having had a drink of water from his bottle and a hunk of bread, lay down with his head on the stone pillow. His big stick was handy, ready to clobber anything that came to interfere with him.

The noises of the night around him were nothing compared to the turmoil of his thoughts, haunting thoughts he'd had all day as he'd walked. Now here he was, God's chosen leader, a fugitive, running away from his angry brother. And yet . . . and yet this morning he'd left the camp like a conquering hero, everyone wishing him well—Esau included.

A couple of tears rolled onto Jacob's unusual pillow-case when he thought about his mother. O for the day when he'd be back to see her again!

(Jacob wasn't to know it tonight, but he'd never see his dear mother Rebekah again. Never.)

"My mother said God told her before I was born that He'd chosen me to be the next leader of His people, after my father is gone. I do want to serve God and lead His people, but tonight, miles from home, I feel frightened and muddled. I don't know God the way Grandfather Abraham knew Him. Father knows God a bit, but not like Grandfather Abraham, either. I wish I knew God."

More tears rolled onto Jacob's strange pillowcase. He was very tired. He'd tramped all day. Now the hootings seemed farther away. The lions' roars, the hyenas' laughter, were being left behind, farther and farther and farther behind. Jacob was asleep!

I don't know how long Jacob had slept before he began to dream. It was still night, of course. But he was having a wonderful time, watching and listening to the things he saw.

As he looked, there was a light—a beautiful beam of light, like you see from the moon when you're standing at the lakeside at night. You've seen it—the light comes right to your feet at the water's edge. You know what I mean. Well, Jacob saw a beautiful beam of light coming down right to where he was. And as he followed it with his eyes up and up and up and up, it reached right into heaven! It looked like a golden staircase or ladder.

Oh, wait a minute! Something moved right at the top of the golden staircase, way up at the top. Whatever was it?

Beautiful. Shining. Moving so gracefully down the ladder. And another following. And another. And another. Quite a procession. Down, down the beautiful, shining ladder. Angels! Yes, it was a procession of angels.

They were so light and graceful and beautiful and peaceful. They came very close to Jacob, almost touching him, where he lay there at the bottom of the ladder. Calm, peaceful, gracious, shining angels! Glorious!

Would any of them speak to him? No, each one looked at him with infinite love, and then, without stopping an instant, walked up the ladder again.

It was a glorious sight now. Angels walking up and down the shining ladder whose top reached right into heaven. None spoke. Jacob was thrilled, elated by the sight. And they all seemed to be his friends. They all seemed to care, but they never said a word.

His eyes had gotten used to the glorious light now, the light of the broad shining ray where the ladder was. Yes, his eyes had gotten used to the light and the glorious glow of the angels. His spirit was calm, even though he was elated. His eyes had traveled up the ladder again—up, up, up. Then, right at the top, he saw a light more brilliant than ever—*a person!*

No! Not a person way up there? Yes, a person!

"Jacob!" the voice said.

What a voice! Rich and melodious—echoing down the beautiful ladder, with the angels walking up and down, up and down. They all stopped walking now at the sound of the voice. They stood quietly, with heads slightly bowed. It was a voice you just had to listen to.

No, no, it didn't make you afraid. Just terribly thrilled, with an out-of-this-world kind of feeling.

"Jacob!" (Oh, listen!) "Jacob, I am the Lord God of your father Abraham, and the God of Isaac. The ground you're lying on is yours. I'm going to give it to your

18

descendants. Your descendants will be as many as the dust, too many to count. They will spread into the lands to the north, and the south, to the east and to the west. And all the nations of the world will be blessed through you and your descendants. Furthermore, I will be with you and protect you wherever you go. I'll look after you and bring you back safely to this land. I will be with you always. And I'll see to it that everything I've promised you will come to pass."

Jacob couldn't have spoken if he'd tried. He was awestruck, looking, listening.

As the tones of the rich, melodious voice echoed and then melted away, the angels on the shining, golden staircase began to walk again. But they were all walking up now. Up, up, up, as if they'd been called back.

Was the light getting fainter? Jacob blinked. Yes! No! Yes, yes, the light was fading.

The light had faded. The ladder and the shining angels were gone!

Jacob woke up.

What a vision he'd had! He trembled. "God was here!" he said. "God *is* here. *This* is the house of God. This is the very door of heaven."

And Jacob got up early in the morning and took the big smooth stone he'd covered with his cloth to make a pillow last night and set it up on end to make a pillar, a monument.

Then he rummaged in his pack and found a little flask of oil he'd brought. (You needed oil when you traveled, for your cuts or sore feet—just as we take our first-aid kit on our journeys today.)

Jacob poured a little of the oil from his flask over the stone pillar he'd set up, and he gave the place a new name.

I told you it was called Luz. Now Jacob renamed it Bethel, which means house of God or God's house.

As he did this, Jacob vowed a vow—a very special promise. He made the vow to God, though Jacob didn't dare to address God personally, not at first. But God was listening all right.

This is what Jacob said: "If God will really help me and protect me on this journey, and give me food to eat and clothes to wear, and bring me back again to my father's house in peace and safety, then I will choose Jehovah to be my God. And this memorial stone will become a place for worshiping Jehovah. And God," he finished up, now speaking to God directly, "I will give You back a tenth of everything that You give to me."

Then Jacob ate some breakfast (a bit of bread and some raisins and a drink from his water bottle) and set off on his journey once more, heading north for his Uncle Laban's place in Haran.

2

The Well of the Magic Words

Now when God calls down out of heaven to Tom, Dick, or Harry, or Mary Jane, or you or me, He doesn't just say things like "Have a nice day!" It's usually a very important message that God has for Tom, Dick, or Harry, or Mary Jane, or you or me. Very important. Something they really need to know, something we really need to know. Maybe for today or tomorrow—for life.

And when God called down to Jacob at Bethel, God had something to say that Jacob was going to need to know and remember. "I will be with you," God said.

You remember that Jacob was lonely and sad and frightened that first night he was away from home, out in the wilds among the rocks.

And you remember how God called to him from the very top of the shining ladder, the golden staircase where the angels were walking up and down. Well, when I read that story, I said to myself, "Jacob is special!"

I know his mother thought so. But now *God* is saying it. "Jacob is special."

I did think, though: "But, God, *is* Jacob worth all this attention? You know he's a fraud—Oh, excuse me, I shouldn't have said that!" I remembered that God chooses *us,* and we've all got a bit of the fraud in us. God chooses us not for what we are, but for what He's going to make of us.

"Right," I thought, "God must be going to make something of Jacob, to pick him out like this for a special message."

"I will be with you, Jacob," God said. "I will bless you, guide you, protect you wherever you go until. . . ."

I read on in our story a bit. "Oh, dear!" I said. You see, Jacob got mixed up with a most ruthless man, uncle or not, father-in-law-to-be or not. And Jacob had one of the most ghastly tricks played on him that I've ever heard of in my life. A cruel, cruel trick.

"Well," I said to myself as I read on in the story, "if ever anybody needed to know that God was keeping an eye on things, Jacob did!"

Let me tell you the story.

It was early in the afternoon when Jacob got to Haran, nearly 450 miles from home. It had been a long walk. There lay the town, sprawled out in front of him, with pasture lands round about. At the outskirts of the city, the first thing Jacob came upon was a well.

Would you believe it? It was the well of the magic words. Jacob's mother it was who'd said those magic words when she was just a girl, sixty years ago. She'd said them to the good old scout Eliezer, who'd been sent on a wife-hunt for Isaac. And the moment the good old scout heard Rebekah's magic words, he just knew God had picked her out to be Isaac's wife.* (She became Jacob's mother later.)

*Look for this story in Come, Meet Abraham, God's Friend.

25

And now Jacob was remembering that story as he looked at that same well.

At the well that afternoon were three flocks of sheep, a few goats, and a couple of little donkeys, all waiting to be given a drink of water from the well. They were bothered by flies and bugs biting them. Vultures wheeled overhead. Vultures seemed to know when there were weak sheep among the flocks, and they wanted to be ready when the poor creatures would fall by the wayside.

The shepherds lolled lazily beside the flocks. It was siesta time, I suppose.

But Jacob wasn't in a siesta mood. Everything was new and strange to him—exciting and challenging.

Today he would meet the relatives he'd never seen. Uncle Laban's family. What would the *girls* of the family be like? Beautiful? Plain? He had no money, so he could not pay his uncle the price for a bride, whoever she

was. His own father, Isaac, hadn't given him a cent when he left home. But the prospect of meeting the girls was exciting to Jacob. And of course, still in his mind, quite vividly, Jacob had the memory and feel of his special dream.

He couldn't forget that God had spoken to him the other night. Picked him out and given him a special promise. If Jacob felt a little "bouncy" this afternoon, you couldn't blame him, could you?

"Hi, chaps," he said to the shepherds. "Where do you come from?"

"We're from these parts—Haran. Where do you think, with all these sheep?"

"Haran?" said Jacob. "Is that a fact? Do you happen to know Laban, the son of a man called Nahor?"

"Yeah, we know him."

"Do you really?" Jacob felt excited. "How is he? Is he well?"

"Sure, he's well enough. Why, his daughter Rachel brings Laban's sheep to this well every day. She'll probably be along here soon."

"Oh," said Jacob, getting even more excited. He squatted beside the shepherds.

"How long do you sit here before you give your flocks water?" he asked. "Why don't you get on with the job now so the animals can go off and eat some more grass? It's far too early in the day for them to have to stop grazing while they wait to be watered. The poor things will be hungry. They won't get enough to keep them going today. And you go on like this every day, not giving them enough grazing time, and you'll have animals in very poor condition."

Jacob was a real shepherd at heart. The lazy attitude of these fellows irritated him.

"Come on," he said again. "Why don't you give the sheep water now so they can go off and eat some more grass before sundown?"

"What, us? *Us* take the stone off the top of this here well? Not us! *Somebody* will take the stone off the top o' the well when *all* the flocks get here. We'll just sit and wait till they all get here."

"Then there'll be a real mess, I should think," said Jacob. "How can hundreds of sheep all drink at once from these few troughs and this one well? The time you waste! And, more important, you're wasting the animals' grazing time! Poor animals!"

Jacob was horrified at the condition of the miserable creatures—thirsty and hungry. Some were even sick, really wretched.

"We can't do nothin' about it. We'd be in trouble if we was to interfere with the rules of the well. We're first on the list for the water. We made sure we was here first. We've been here a long time already. But we daren't touch that stone on the top of the well. We surely daren't. Can't expect us to do that. When they all get here—the flocks—then'll be the time for waterin'."

Jacob was disgusted. He opened his mouth to say something but—

"Hi, young fella," another shepherd chipped in, "wasn't you askin' about Laban, son of Nahor, a minute ago? See that flock coming over there? That's his. And that's his gal Rachel. She looks after her father's sheep. Pretty little miss, she is. If she was my gal, I wouldn't have her lookin' after my sheep. I'd take care o' her. Nice little gal!"

Jacob gazed eagerly at the flock that was coming towards the well, led by the dainty shepherdess.

He was about to say to the shepherd, "You're sure she's Laban's daughter, are you?" But he didn't need to. As he saw her face more clearly, he could see that the beautiful Rachel looked very much like his own mother, Rebekah. The family likeness was remarkable.

Jacob fell in love with Rachel on the spot. Talk about love at first sight!

For a moment he said nothing to her except, "I'll water your flocks." He just had to do something.

To the utter astonishment of the shepherds, Jacob shoved the great stone from the mouth of the well, drew the water, and splashed it into the troughs for his Uncle Laban's sheep.

Rachel stood by speechless. She liked this kind stranger who broke all the well rules and picked her flock out for watering.

In no time Jacob had finished drawing the water and splashing it into the troughs. And while the sheep were drinking, he looked at Rachel as she stood there beside her sheep. She looked so sweet and so like his mother. Jacob just couldn't help it—he went and kissed her cheek. Before she could protest or run away (if she wanted to), this strange man was crying like a baby.

"I'm Rebekah's son," he said, "your Aunt Rebekah's son. I'm your cousin Jacob!"

"Oh," she said. "Let me go and tell dad!"

So off ran Rachel, blushing like anything, to tell her dad.

In a short time Laban came running. He hugged Jacob and kissed him and excitedly took him home. How Uncle Laban welcomed Jacob into his home.

"You're my own flesh and blood," he said, "my own sister's son! Well! Well! Welcome, Jacob!"

3

Uncle Laban

When Jacob's uncle had gotten over the surprise of seeing him, he put two and two together, even before they reached the house. And he said to himself, "This fella is looking for a wife, I'll be bound. What else would bring him way up here to Haran? Years ago Abraham sent up here for my sister Rebekah to be Isaac's wife. Now, I guess, Rebekah and Isaac have sent Jacob up here to look for a wife for himself. Same tale, I suppose—no suitable girls around where they live. Yes, that'll be it. He's looking for a wife. But the fella came on foot, with nothing in his hand but his small pack and his stick. He brings no presents, no money, seemingly. Well, well! We shall see what we shall see."

Right now Jacob needed a place to live, and he decided to stay with his Uncle Laban. His uncle's welcome seemed most kind.

Jacob met his boy cousins and his other girl cousin, Leah. Leah was like Rachel in many ways, particularly in height and build. You could tell at a glance that Rachel and Leah were sisters, but Leah's eyes were not bright and beautiful like Rachel's. Leah was in charge of the food for the household. Rachel was the outdoor girl, the shepherdess.

As Rachel talked to her sheep, her voice was music to Jacob's ears. Watching the wind blow her curls till they danced round her pretty face sent ecstatic shivers down Jacob's spine.

Rachel was so like her Aunt Rebekah, Jacob's mother, that he couldn't take his eyes off her. He'd fallen head over heels in love with his cousin Rachel. And Rachel was soon head over heels in love with Jacob. Very exciting!

But Jacob didn't have a penny to offer her father for a bride price. Just nothing.

If a message had come right then from Rebekah, "Jacob, come home, son. It's all clear now. Esau isn't angry any more," what would Jacob have done? I'll tell you. He wouldn't have wanted to go—not without

Rachel. And he couldn't go *with* her because he had no money to make her his wife.

For a month, this was how matters stood. And Laban's family wasn't blind. They saw just how things were with Jacob and Rachel.

Leah, by the way, had also fallen in love with her cousin Jacob. But Jacob didn't want her attentions. What a nuisance!

Jacob's uncle knew a good thing when he saw it, and he saw in Jacob a first-class shepherd. What Jacob didn't know about sheep rearing wasn't worth knowing. Laban saw a great future for his business, with Jacob to direct it.

Laban didn't want to lose Jacob. "Better offer him some wages. That'll keep him here. Can't think why he should arrive here penniless. We were told Abraham had great riches. I heard that old servant, Eliezer, say so myself. And the gifts he brought! Well, anyway, this chap Jacob needs money. I'll offer to pay him to keep him. Also, if I pay, I call the shots."

"Jacob," Laban said to him later, "you know, just because we're related doesn't mean that you should work for me for nothing. I'll pay you wages. Tell me, what wages do you want?"

"I'll work for you for seven years if at the end of the seven years you'll allow me to marry Rachel, Uncle," Jacob said.

"Well," said Laban, "come to think of it, I'd rather give my daughter to you than to a stranger. Okay! Jacob, you work for me for seven years, and at the end you shall have my daughter to be your wife."

So that was settled. Jacob would have a home for seven years with his uncle and the promise that the girl he loved would be his wife at the end of it.

But that meant Jacob wouldn't be going home during the next seven years. Even if a message should come from his mother that it would be all right, all safe, to come home, Jacob was now bound to stay with his uncle. But what did that matter? He was where Rachel was. And he was the one who set the time at seven years.

And all through the seven years, would you believe it, Leah was deeply in love with Jacob. Yes, she was. Poor girl, she didn't stand a ghost of a chance, because Jacob loved Rachel— had loved her ever since the moment he met her at the well. And Rachel loved Jacob.

But there was Leah under the same roof. Always making the meals. Always there. Yes, there was Leah. All through the seven years.

* * * * * * *

When the seven years were nearly up, Jacob began counting the days. He hadn't lost track of the time. Oh, no! However, Laban didn't ever say at supper or dinner, "Well, Jacob, the seven years are nearly up. I'm arranging the marriage feast." Not a bit of it! Laban didn't say anything of the kind. Whenever was he going to mention it?

Rachel had her wedding clothes ready, hoping that any day the wedding would be announced. But never a word about it from her father.

40

Girls then, as now, had their hope chests, where they stored veils and perfumes and make-up for their wedding day—their trousseaus, too. Rachel had hers ready. I suppose Leah also had her hope chest ready. You never knew when a suitor would arrive with ten camels laden with gifts and robes and gems!

It was like listening to a fairy tale to hear about the time when the camels came for Aunt Rebekah unexpectedly, out of the blue—late one afternoon.*And by morning she was riding away to her wedding. Good thing she'd had her hope chest ready, wasn't it? And her nurse Deborah had gone away with her. Deborah's relatives were still living in Haran.

It had been the talk of the town—Prince Charming's ambassador coming like that (Prince Charming was Isaac, remember?). Oh, yes, if you were a girl in those days, you never knew when your Prince Charming would show up. Any more than girls know today! It's just as exciting today.

As the end of the seven years got nearer, Jacob and Rachel were so excited. But would you believe it? Never a mention of it from Laban. Had he forgotten? Surely Jacob wouldn't have to go and ask him for his wages? It would be most impolite to do that. But he had worked hard for seven whole years. He'd worked gladly, but now he wanted his wages—his bride. But never a word about it from Uncle Laban, his boss.

"The time has come," Jacob said to Rachel one day.

*See *Come, Meet Abraham, God's Friend*

"I'll have to go and ask."

"Uncle Laban," Jacob said. "I have something to talk to you about."

"Sure, Jacob. The flocks? You're doing a good job."

"No, uncle. My wages. Wages."

"Oh, yes, wages. What did we decide upon? What did we arrange? Oh, yes— wages."

"Uncle," Jacob said, "you promised me that at the end of seven years you would give me Rachel to be my wife. Marrying Rachel is my wages. Rachel is my wages. I've worked for you for seven years, uncle. The time is up. Now let me marry Rachel."

"Of course, of course, young fella. We must arrange it for sure. Leave it—leave it with me. I'll—I'll make the arrangements. I'll get on with the job at once."

So Laban sent out invitations to the wedding, and the invitation said simply: "I am marrying my daughter to Jacob, my nephew. The festivities will take place two weeks from now. You are invited to the wedding."

4

The Wrong Bride!

The wedding invitations had gone out. "Come to my daughter's wedding," Laban said. Acceptances were coming in. Jacob and Rachel were excited.

Now a marriage feast lasted for seven days at least, fourteen sometimes. Imagine a party lasting seven days! I know when you're at a party you wish it could go on and on. Well, in the lands of the East, parties did! Delicious food and drinks, music, games, jokes and riddles, and contests. You can't imagine the fun that went on at weddings. Mostly among the men, though. The women were busy preparing it all.

Well, on about the seventh evening of the festivities, the actual wedding usually took place. Let me tell you about the processions. They were fun!

The bridegroom's procession was first.

48

There would be the bridegroom, dressed in his wedding robes. His friends would mount him on a horse and parade him through the town. Torches made of tightly rolled cloth soaked in oil were lit and carried high on poles. The torches flared and spluttered. Some people carried silk lanterns, like Chinese lanterns. The bridegroom had to keep his mouth covered with a part of his robe held in his left hand. He had to be shy and humble.

On another horse, behind the bridegroom, rode a little boy dressed exactly like him. And this little boy had to imitate every movement and action of the bridegroom as they went along. This custom always caused a great deal of merriment. Jacob, as he waited dressed for his wedding, knew what to expect before he'd be escorted to the wedding apartment.

And, of course, Rachel was getting ready too. Underneath her heavy veil, she wore her beautiful wedding dress. It was a gorgeous costly creation, pale gold material, embroidered with gold and silver and silken threads, embellished with brilliant spangles and stones in the form of flower sprays and bouquets.

The train of the dress was six yards long, and the sleeves swept the floor. Rachel's wedding dress had to be really gorgeous. And it was! Masses of orange blossom in the room gave off a most refreshing perfume. She had some wreathed round her hair-do, under her veil. She loved the perfume.

Rachel was ready. She'd be collected just before midnight and taken to the marriage apartment, where Jacob would be waiting for her.

Her procession would be fun too. There'd be torches—coils of oiled cloth, blazing—held high on poles, and silk lanterns, like Chinese lanterns, carried in people's hands. And there'd be a jester clanging on cymbals. The more he carried on as he danced, the more of a fool he looked; and the more he humiliated himself, the more honor he gave to the bride. That's how it would be.

51

Rachel sat alone in her room—waiting.

Well, it was nearly midnight now. She heard a great commotion outside—music, clanging, laughter.

"Oh, that must be Jacob's procession on its way to the marriage apartment. Bursts of applause, merriment, laughter. The little boy on his horse behind Jacob's horse must be doing his stuff. Now the noise has died down somewhat. Oh, Jacob must be there now. Now they'll come for me!"

Rachel pinched herself for joy. She sat alone. Her attendants were outside—waiting for the signal to fetch her.

"Ah, the fun has started up again. Now they're coming for me."

The sounds came closer—but no one came in. Then the noise was really deafening—cymbals clanged, people laughed. Rachel could even hear the torches flaring—she thought. In a moment her attendants would burst in, and she'd be taken to Jacob, who was waiting for her. He'd waited so long—seven years— but in a matter of minutes the long waiting would be over. She and Jacob would be together for always.

But wait! It sounded as if the procession had *passed.* Couldn't be!

"Oh, they'll be back," she told herself. "When folks get merry, they play around a bit. They're teasing me. Soon they'll come back."

Rachel waited breathlessly. In the distance she heard a great shout, cheering, and then the noise died down.

No one came near her door.

"I shouldn't," she said to herself, "not on my wedding night. I shouldn't go outside alone, but I must see what has happened."

And Rachel went to open the door.

It was locked! She was locked in!

"What trick is this?" she said. "To lock me in and tease me so? Whoever has done it? But Jacob will come and look for me himself soon. He knows where I am. As soon as everybody has finally gone to bed, he'll come and get me himself."

And Rachel waited. And waited. And waited. All night. Till dawn came in the eastern sky.

Soon after dawn, Rachel heard a rattling and a banging on her father's door. And she heard Jacob's voice—angry, furious.

"What is this you have done to me?" he stormed. "I served you seven years for Rachel. Last night a bride was brought to me in the dark, and this morning when the daylight came I saw it was Leah! And I've married her!"

Then he seemed to stop being furious, just calmly broken-hearted. (Did he remember something, I wonder? Something that had happened seven years before when he pretended to be Esau. Now Leah had pretended to be Rachel, and he'd married her. Wow! Don't things come home to roost!)

By now Laban was talking. "Keep your shirt on, old chap! What did you expect? You know in these parts it's unheard of to marry a younger sister off before her older one. If someone had come along for Leah in the meantime, well and good. But nobody did. So you had to have her. See?

"Now calm down. Why not have 'em both. If you give me your solemn promise to work for me another seven years, you shall marry Rachel at the end of this week. Okay?"

Did you ever hear anything as callous as that? Laban hadn't put himself in anybody else's shoes. All he'd done was to stand in his own and say, "My business is prospering under Jacob's clever management. He'll go off home the minute he gets Rachel. How can I keep him here?" And he'd thought up this wicked plan. If only he'd known it, Jacob couldn't go home. There was Esau.

Rachel, poor girl, alone in her locked room, had fainted when she heard, "It was Leah! And I've married her!" But as she came to, she heard, "You shall marry Rachel at the end of this week. Okay?" She banged on the locked door.

She heard someone fumbling at the lock. The door opened, and there stood Jacob. He cried like a wounded animal. "My Rachel!" he said. Rachel only sobbed and clung to him.

"I must go," he said. "But at the end of the week, no one shall keep us apart!"

In the meantime, what about Leah? She was married all right—to a man whose love was someone else's. But she adored Jacob.

What a mean trick! Leah had agreed to her father's awful plan. She'd dressed herself for the wedding, just like her sister. And when the bridesmaids came, there she was heavily veiled, waiting for them. Ready—while her sister waited in the locked room.

Well, they all got through the week somehow. And then on the promised day, Jacob went for Rachel himself. No veils or processions this time. And away they went over the hills and far away. They'd come back when they felt like it.

Well, here's a pretty how-do-you-do! We've got something to think out here, haven't we? It wasn't you who said the Bible was dull and boring, was it?

5

Rivals

Well, Jacob and Rachel got back from their honey-moon eventually. They'd been away for weeks. No, they hadn't been to Florida or California, or the Bahamas or Europe, or the Channel Islands, or on safari in Africa. They'd been over the hills and far away on foot, taking Laban's sheep with them to new green pastures.

It wasn't really a hardship at all to take the sheep with them. (It had to be done anyway!) They both loved sheep, understood sheep. Rachel had been her father's shepherdess until Jacob had come along. Now, thanks to Jacob's skill and knowledge—he had all kinds of cures and remedies for sheep—it was a very healthy and contented flock that he and Rachel took with them on their honeymoon.

All summer long Jacob and Rachel had been away with the sheep.

They'd camped beside streams and brooks . . .
under trees . . . and in the open . . . on hillsides . . . in
valleys. The wild flowers had been a riot of color. And
each night the stars had twinkled down at them from a
deep blue, velvet sky.

Marvelous music had filled the air each morning.
Jacob and Rachel had had the birds' dawn chorus to
tell them the time. Then they'd watched the white mist,
lying close to the ground, disperse as suddenly the sun
was with them again, and all the grey turned to gold and
color sprang up all round them once more. They'd
watched the sleeping sheep stir and shake themselves
and start to graze.

All day long Rachel and Jacob wandered slowly with
the sheep. In the lazy afternoons, when the animals lay
and rested in the shade a while, they rested too. There
was no sound except the drone of a few bees, busy
collecting honey.

By evening they'd wended their way to a brook. And,

60

having had their drink of water, the sheep settled for the night. For Jacob and Rachel there was their evening meal, the glorious afterglow of sunset, the talking time before sleep.

The summer had been glorious.

But now there was a nip in the air. Steam rose from the flock as their warm breath met the cold morning air.

"Ah," said Jacob, "now we must go back. But we go back together, my Rachel. God will be with us. He promised me."

Jacob had told Rachel all he knew about God. About the vision at Bethel—the angels on the golden staircase and God actually calling down to him from the top of the ladder. Jacob had had to tell Rachel that story many times—she just couldn't believe it! He'd told her about God calling him and choosing *him* to be the leader of God's people. And about the great Deliverer who was coming one day through the family somewhere—way down the family line, in the future.

Now as they turned their faces homeward, Jacob said, "It's not the way I would have had it, my Rachel. I only meant to marry you—you know that. I had Leah thrust upon me; your father did it. We'll just have to make the best of it. I must do my duty, Rachel. But you'll know that you have all my love."

Well, they got home with the sheep.
There was Leah. And the fight was on.
"He's mine!" Leah said.
"No, he's mine!" said Rachel.
Of course, when God created the world, He'd only given Adam one wife. And all the things God said at the time of creation showed that that's how He meant it to be: one man—one wife. But you know from our stories so far that people got away from what God said and made their own customs, which they thought would be fun. Even God's people got mixed up with these customs and copied the people living round them. And, of course, it didn't make them happy.

Remember in Abraham's story the fuss there was about Hagar?* Poor Princess Sarah had a time of it, didn't she?

"Yes," you say, "and her own fault!"

Quite so. Princess Sarah was copying a pagan custom to have her maid Hagar have a son for her. The custom was considered respectable and legal, but, of course, man's customs and laws are sometimes far from God's standards.

I have to tell you that we're going to hear some more

*See *Come, Meet Abraham, the Pioneer.*

62

about that custom
in this story.
When a girl
got married
in those days,
part of her
wedding present
from her father
was a handmaid,
a personal maid.
This maid
was so personal
that she
could even
have children
for her mistress.
Rachel had
her personal maid
called Bilhah,
and Leah's
personal maid
was called Zilpah.

Now, to us in Christian Era this custom is unthinkable. But in Jacob's time people thought the custom was all right, so we must take them as we find them. Man's customs and laws are sometimes far from God's standards. And let's watch the kind and gracious way that God loved them and helped them when they tried to serve Him, even through their mistakes.

Well, now, here's Jacob with two wives, Rachel and Leah. The Bible tells us he hated Leah. Now I wouldn't be at all surprised if he had hated her, but we must remember that "hated" here means "loved less." So I don't think for a minute that Jacob hated Leah; he just loved Leah less than Rachel. Rachel was *the* one.

The story isn't pretty, but it's real and true. Leah tried so hard to be *the* one in Jacob's eyes. When her first son, Reuben, was born, she was thrilled to bits. "Now what will Jacob say to this? A son! Rachel doesn't have any sons yet." She didn't have any daughters either, but sons counted most. (Sorry about that, girls!)

Well, we won't go into all the details, but by the time Leah had had four sons, Reuben, Simeon, Levi, and Judah, she was very excited. "Jacob is sure to love me better than Rachel now," Leah said. But no. Jacob didn't say so.

When her sister Leah had four sons and she had none, Rachel got very upset and very jealous. She cried a lot. She cried bitterly to Jacob, "If I don't have a son, I'll die!"

Jacob was horrified to hear his Rachel talking like that. "I am not God," he told her. "It is God who has not given you a son."

But there was no comforting Rachel. "Jacob," she said. "I must have a son!" So she suggested that her personal maid, Bilhah, should have a son for her. And Bilhah did. She had Dan, which made Rachel very happy. Then Bilhah had another son, Naphtali. (I'm telling you their names because you're going to hear of them again.)* Dan and Naphtali were counted as belonging to Rachel.

Now although Leah had four sons and Rachel two, Leah couldn't bear to think that she was only two ahead of her sister. So now she suggested that *her* maid, Zilpah, should have a son or two. And Zilpah did. She had Gad and Asher. Leah was glad to add two more sons, Gad and Asher, to her total—making six now.

*See *Come, Meet Joseph, God's Dreamer* and *Come, Meet Joseph, the Grand Vizier.*

But some people are never satisfied. And as time went on, Leah thought six sons were not enough. So she asked God to please give her more sons. God listened, and she had Issachar and Zebulun. Not twins—Issachar first, then Zebulun. That brought her grand total to eight.

She still hoped for another but, believe it or not, next time she got a girl. Dinah. You'll hear of Dinah again. Poor girl! There was an awful row about Dinah, but that was later.* Right now Dinah's arrival made Leah thankful that she had eight boys to her credit.

*See *Come, Meet Jacob, God's Prince.*

So we don't hear Leah saying very much right now. She had nine children to look after, a lot to do even with Zilpah's help. And she still had to cook for her dad, Laban, and her brothers. (Jacob ate most of his meals with Rachel.) Yes, Leah had enough to do.

Rachel was pleased with Dan and Naphtali, the two boys Bilhah had had for her. But she was still longing to have a son of her very own, however often Jacob told her that he loved her for herself.

She tried to eat the right things (whatever they were), took her vitamins, and all—and prayed. Then one day . . . Well! Well! . . .

"Jacob," she said, "I believe I'm going to have a son for you at last."

And she did. And listen! His name was JOSEPH.

Rachel didn't know what a favorite he was going to be with us. Oh, yes, he was a favorite with his dad, Jacob, too.* In some ways that was too bad. But he's a great favorite with us.

I knew you'd love to know about Joseph being born. Well, he was born in Haran, Mesopotamia. And Rachel was his mother.

Now, let's pass by Laban's family home where they all live. See the tents and houses and sheep pens, cattle and camels and donkeys, just outside the sophisticated city of Haran. Oh, yes, and the well of the magic words too.

See those ten boys around Laban's place!

The two together, like inseparable twins, are probably Simeon and Levi. Those two are always in trouble together.

*See *Come, Meet Joseph, God's Dreamer.*

And that group of four, like a gang, are probably Dan and Asher, Gad and Naphtali. Those four are the handmaids' sons, Zilpah's and Bilhah's. They sort of stick together. They feel their rating isn't quite as high as Jacob's other sons. They know it has to do with their mothers, so they stick together in a bunch.

Reuben, of course, acts the oldest of the lot, and there's Zebulun. And Judah—he looks special.

Take a peep at baby Joseph, if you can. He's very small—just a baby right now—and he'll probably be asleep.

6
Two Schemers

Everything Jacob touched turned to gold. Everything! But the gold was for his father-in-law, Laban, his boss. Not a penny for himself. Jacob was just as penniless now as he'd been the day he first arrived in Haran with nothing but his shepherd's crook.

That was fourteen years ago, at least, and Jacob had never been home to Hebron since. Now he wanted to go home.

So he said to his Uncle Laban, who was also his father-in-law and practically owned him by now, "I want to go home. I want to go back to see my old dad, Isaac. I want to go back to Hebron, where I belong."

71

For years now Jacob had slogged and slaved for his ruthless, scheming father-in-law, Laban.

For seven long years, Jacob had worked hard to pay for Rachel to be his wife. And he'd done it gladly. He'd known that he'd have to work to pay for a bride since he had no money. All he had was his shepherd's staff—a sign of his skill as a shepherd. Yes, he'd known he'd have to work to pay some father for a daughter to be his wife, but to be tricked at the end of the time was cruel beyond words.

He'd been landed with Leah. But he'd taken his disappointment and stuck it out, slogging another seven years for Rachel, whom he loved most dearly.

Now he had eleven sons and at least one daughter, Dinah. And when the eleventh son, Joseph, was born to his darling wife Rachel, Jacob said to Laban: "I want to go home, back to see my old dad, and back to where I belong. I want to take my children and Rachel—and Leah, of course—with me. I've worked for them. They're mine."

"Oh, no! Don't go! Stay with us. Whatever do you want to do that for? I can't hear of that!"

Then Laban turned really religious. "You know, Jacob," he said, "I'm quite sure that God has blessed me because of you. You've been a real blessing here."

Well! Skinflint Laban wasn't going to let a good workman go! And didn't he know the right thing to say?

Polishing up Jacob's halo like that!

"Oh, of course, you should have some wages from me, now that you've paid for my daughters. Tell me, son, what shall your wages be? Name a figure, a price. I'll pay you."

Jacob thought a moment. He also had the Laban trait in him—the twisty family trait.

"Well, uncle, father-in-law, you know how I've looked after your flocks and herds. They were little and scrawny enough when I came, and now look at them—hordes of 'em, multitudes of good healthy animals. And, as you say, the Lord has blessed you since I came. But, uncle, when do you suggest that I begin to gather something together for my own lot? I've got a houseful, if anybody has. Isn't it about time?"

"Well, Jacob, name a price, a wage. I'll give it. You shall have what you ask. What do you want me to give you?"

"You shan't give me anything, uncle. Nothing!"

Laban's mouth dropped open. Was he going to lose this gold-maker?

Jacob went on:

"But there is something you can do for me. If you do it, I will stay with you and look after your flocks and herds."

Laban's eyes brightened. He shut his mouth that had dropped open with disappointment a moment ago.

He listened as Jacob went on: "I will pick over your flocks and take out all the spotted and speckled sheep and all the black lambs, and all the spotted and speckled goats—the mongrels. And I'll put all these mongrels in a place by themselves, and they shall be my wages. They spoil the look of your flocks anyway. Furthermore, when these animals that shall be mine have pure-looking young ones, I will hand them over to you to go into your flocks. How's that?"

"Right you are, Jacob!" Laban said. He heaved a sigh of relief. He was going to be able to keep his great shepherd and manager, the man with the golden touch, after all. And Jacob hadn't asked much. Mongrels were few and far between.

"Done it!" Laban smirked as he pulled up a grass stalk.

He chewed on that grass stalk all the way over to his house. "Ah, but what's he up to now, though? . . . Huh? . . . 'I'll pick over the flocks,' he said, didn't he? No, no, Jacob, my boy. I'll pick over the flocks myself in the morning. What's more, my friend, your speckled and striped and whatever, and blacks and browns, will be in the charge of my own boys. Eh? Ha, ha! And they shall be removed from my flocks three days' journey— forty miles.

"No, no, Jacob, grabber, none of your monkey tricks, m'lad. Your animals shall not eat grass that mine need. And when we've got your striped, speckled, and what-ever right out of the way, I'll know that you can't breed any more mongrels from my herd. Got ya there, grab-ber! Ha! Ha! Ha!"

Laban did not, of course, say this all out loud to Jacob—just to himself. But Jacob didn't need to hear it. Actions speak louder than words.

However, Jacob settled down again and agreed to keep working for Laban for these new wages. All the speckled, striped and spotted sheep and goats and all the black sheep would be his wages.

And life went on again. I did tell you that everything Jacob touched turned to gold. But within his family it was more like iron. Cold, hard iron. Jealousy, envy, fighting. The ladies were often at it, fighting over Jacob. And the children quarreled too.

Well, Jacob began to get rich, now that he had his

own flocks and herds—speckled and spotted and striped or not. Good fat animals. He could trade wool and butter and cheese. Yes, Jacob was getting richer every day now.

If any of his flocks produced white offspring, he gave those of a pure color to Laban, his uncle, just as he said he would. But if any of Laban's pure-colored animals had speckled or spotted or striped offspring, they were sent to Jacob's flocks, forty miles away. How's that? Fair? Sounds fine!

Well, of course, you can't be surprised that Jacob, being a shrewd businessman as well as a good shepherd, hoped that Uncle Laban's pure-colored goats and sheep would have babies that were striped or spotted or speckled and that there would be some black lambs born. And there were.

Jacob also hoped and planned that these spotted, speckled, and striped goats and sheep would be strong and healthy. And they were.

Jacob knew a bit about what is called selective breeding. And he also had the idea that if the mothers looked long enough at spotted and speckled objects, their young would be spotted and speckled. So Jacob cut sticks from the trees and peeled the bark off in patterns, leaving white spots—spotty. On some sticks he cut the bark in strips—stripy.

Whether there was any magic power in what he did, I wouldn't know, but it worked! Spots and stripes were the order of the day. (Later, he said God told him what to do and controlled everything. That is more like it, I would think.)

Anyway, nearly all the baby goats and sheep being born were spotted, striped, or speckled, and there were many black lambs.

Laban got quite upset. "Uh—uh—uh—what—what's this? Too much, too much."

Laban was careful in what he said though. He still didn't want to lose his good workman. But he would set a limit. "Jacob," he said, "this is too much of a good thing for you; too much of a bad thing for me. Now I

79

know you'll be
reasonable. Let us
say that this year the
striped goats and
the black sheep are
for you. All the rest
for me."

"All right," Jacob said, however he felt about it.

Lo and behold, masses of striped goats were born—and black lambs!

"Well, well," said Laban, who was keeping an eye on everything and being very "honest." Jacob also was being very "honest." God was blessing them *both,* so they said.

"Now, Jacob, be reasonable. I know you will." (Laban didn't want to lose Jacob.) "All these striped animals for you and nothing much for me this year? Now next year you just can have the speckled and spotted, and I'll have the striped. Okay?"

"Sure, uncle," said Jacob. And would you believe it, in the springtime, you never saw so many baby animals with speckled and spotted coats as were born in Laban's flocks.

Laban made a new rule for the next springtime, and the next, still trying to keep Jacob, and still trying not to let himself be ruined.

It was good that Jacob had so many big boys growing up, because his flocks increased greatly.

Jacob made money, hired servants, bought manservants and maidservants, bought camels and donkeys. Jacob was rich.

But Rachel and Leah were still fighting. There were family quarrels all the time.

Then Laban began to get snarky. I'm not surprised, are you? His animals were not doing so well now. His sons were griping and grumbling and saying: "Jacob is ruining our dad. Building up his own flocks. Feathering his own nest. Jacob has become well-known and honored in these parts. But what he's got, he's gotten from our dad." They were snarky, too.

Jacob felt uncomfortable. He looked at Laban's face. It was dark, scheming, threatening.

Just at this time, God said, "Jacob, it's time to go home now, back to Hebron. I'm your God. I spoke to you at Bethel. Remember? I've kept My word to you. Now, go home!"

So Jacob told Rachel and Leah about it. "Let's go out and talk in the field," he said.

So the three of them went out into the middle of the field where there were no bushes or trees for anyone to hide behind and listen. "Your dad is through with me now," Jacob said. "And your brothers are quite horrid. In any case, God has told me that we must now go home, back to Hebron."

"It's fine with us," Rachel and Leah said. "We've nothing to gain by staying around here. Father doesn't treat us like daughters at all. He sold us to you, and he's never given us a penny. And we won't get anything now. The sooner we're out of his grasp, the better. When do we start? The promise that God will be with us is comforting. Any time you say, Jacob, we'll be ready to go."

And they were!

7

Jacob Makes a Getaway

When you've really made up your mind to do something, it's amazing how you can get it done, even though it seems impossible.

Jacob had made up his mind to go home. Back to Hebron. Back to see his old dad, Isaac. (Isaac was still alive, would you believe it? And years ago he'd talked of dying soon. You never know, do you?)

Now, Jacob knew that when he left Haran and his Uncle Laban, there was going to be a row, a great big row, because Laban had no intention of losing his top shepherd and expert business manager, who was also his son-in-law.

Not only that. Jacob now had a huge family. Eleven sons—some of the older ones were in charge of the flocks. He had one daughter we know of, Dinah, and maybe others that are not mentioned. There was his darling wife Rachel. And there was Leah, of course. And the maids. And servants of all kinds, and their children. And hundreds of animals. And think of the food they would need to take for the long journey.

"It's going to be some job to get this caravan on the road," Jacob must have said. "But we'll do it."

It was the beginning of summer by the time Jacob had gotten everything thought out, and the grass was growing green, so there'd be food for the animals as they traveled.

And just then Laban decided that he'd go over to where some of his sheep were grazing some miles away and supervise the shearing. Their wool was valuable, and he wanted to keep an eye on things way over there. Servants packed food for Laban and his helpers, and away they all went to the sheepshearing. Sheepshearing time was a merry time. Laban was in good spirits.

As soon as Laban and his helpers were gone, Jacob gave the word: "Now's the time! Away we go!"

Ten miles a day would be about as far as the caravan could travel. Everything was planned carefully, and the older boys keeping the sheep and goats miles away met up with the others. Soon they were all on their way—back to Hebron, back to see Isaac.

Jacob and his family had been gone three days from Haran, and Laban, still away supervising his wool business, didn't know a thing.

"Fine wool you've got there, Laban!" a neighboring sheep owner said. "You'll have to tell us how you do it. My sheep now, their wool is worm-eaten. I don't believe you've got a single wool worm in your whole flock, Laban."

"No, don't believe I have. Not a one," Laban said.

"You'll have to tell us how you do it, Laban. You've got a secret there. You might share it with us," his neighbor said.

"Well, you know," Laban said, "to be perfectly honest with you, I don't know what it is myself. My nephew, son-in-law Jacob—he's the one who knows all there is to know about sheep rearing and shepherding. I know I'm lucky to have him. When he first came here, I was afraid he'd be off home again in the first month. But by hook and by crook, I've kept him here these twenty years, and believe me, I've no intention of letting him go. First class he is."

"From what I hear, though," the neighbor went on, "he's been feathering his own nest pretty well lately. Prominent man in these parts, too. Respected is Jacob."

Another shearer passing by with a pack of wool on his back said, "Heard the latest? Jacob, Laban's nephew, son-in-law, has moved. Been gone three days. His old skinflint uncle—"

"Jacob gone?" Laban howled. "Jacob—"

"Oh, beg pardon, Laban. Didn't notice it was you, with this here great pack of wool on my back. I'm just about bent over."

Laban looked terrible. "Jacob gone, did you say? Who told you?"

"Man came through here on his camel—just mentioned it in passing. He assured me it was true when I questioned him."

Laban was furious. He dashed over to his servants. "Look after the sheep," he said to one group. To another, "We must catch him. After Jacob! Quick! Stop him! Catch him!"

They stopped at the farm on the way just to check. "Yes, Jacob went last week."

"What's he stolen?" Laban must find out what Jacob had stolen. How Laban trusted Jacob!

"Gone!" he yelled. "My images. Thinks he's my heir, if he has my household gods, does he? Get him!"

And Laban was off again in hot pursuit. No need to ask which way they went. All those animals belonging to Jacob left tracks behind them.

Laban was furious. At night when they stopped for rest, he could hardly sleep, he was so angry. What he wouldn't do to Jacob!

But then he cooled down. "Ah," he said to himself, "I will persuade him to return. He shall ask what he likes. I will *persuade* him!" Laban got quite sentimental over his daughters, Rachel and Leah, and his grandchildren. Useful boys they were anyway.

Whether by being smooth and pleasant Laban could

have persuaded Jacob to go back with him or not, I don't know. But he didn't get the chance, because during the night God spoke to Laban, Jacob's father-in-law.

"Don't you dare say anything to Jacob," God said, "neither good nor bad. No persuading. No threats. Merely say good-by."

That was a surprise to Laban. He didn't like the message, but perhaps he felt honored to be picked out to be spoken to by God.

Well, on the seventh day of traveling, Laban and his men caught up with Jacob and his caravan. They were in the hills of Gilead, pitched for the night.

"Jacob," he said, "whatever made you steal away like this, as if you were fleeing from a battle with booty? Fancy taking my daughters away as if they were captives. Why didn't you tell me you were going? We could have had a party—song and dance and merriment and

friends. You didn't even give me a chance to kiss my daughters and grandchildren good-by. What a silly thing to do. Fancy running away from me.

"Now, I could do you a lot of harm. But last night your God spoke to me. Told me not to say anything to you, good or bad, so I'm not saying it. I know that you're homesick for your dad and all that, but tell me—why have you stolen my household gods, my images?"

"Images? What would I want with your images? The reason I left the way I did was because I was afraid you'd take your daughters away from me by force. As for your images, I certainly haven't got them. Nor has anyone here."

Jacob felt sure it was just an excuse for Laban to go through all the stuff to see what they had taken with them—nosy, suspicious man.

"You can search for your images," Jacob said. "As if we'd want them! And if anyone has them, let that person die." (Jacob had no idea that Rachel had stolen them.)

So Laban began his search. He came to search in Jacob's tent. No images. Leah's tent. No images. Zilpah's tent and Bilhah's tent. No images. Rachel's tent.

There sat Rachel on the saddle chair that she rode in
on her camel.

"I'm looking for my images," Laban said.

"Oh, daddy, hunt away. But do excuse me for not
getting up. I'm not feeling well today."

The images were hidden in the saddle bag. But nobody ever knew except Rachel, who was sitting on that
saddle chair in her tent.

So Laban never found his images.

"There you are!" Jacob said. "I told you nobody here had them. You just wanted an excuse to search everything. Why did you rush after me like this, as if I was a bandit? Let everybody come and look over anything. As if I'd steal from you! If I had wanted to steal, many a time I could have done it!

"Instead, I bore the loss of your animals eaten by wolves and torn by wild beasts. I needn't have. But I did. I slaved day and night for you, caring for your flocks in the summer drought and heat and in the winter frost, and you changed my wages ten times.

"If it hadn't been that God was helping me, even now, I'd have nothing. God has seen how you've treated me, and He's told you off—last night."

"Jacob," Laban said, "these women are my daughters. These children are my grandchildren. These cattle are my cattle. But what can I do? Come, let's made a covenant, an agreement, a peace pact."

Jacob said to his older boys, "Gather stones." So they did. "Pile 'em up here," he said. They did.

"Now look," Laban said, "this heap of stones is a witness between us. Don't you dare come past here to fight against me. And I promise not to come past here to fight against you. May the Lord watch between you and me while we are out of each other's sight. We sure can't trust each other. We must have God to keep watch over us and judge us."

And so the name of the place was called Mizpah— which means "watchtower."

Then Laban went on: "Promise that you'll look after my daughters and not have any wives except them. And be good to the children. God is watching you!"

(Well, well Laban! You've got a guilty conscience about your daughters, haven't you?)

That night Jacob offered a sacrifice to God; he made a great roast and invited Laban and his men to the feast.

In the morning, Laban kissed his daughters and grandchildren good-by and went back home to Haran.

And Jacob and his company set out again for Hebron.

Be sure to read more about Jacob in the next book in this series—*Come, Meet Jacob, God's Prince.*